W9-BID-430

Amelia Bedelia
and the
Surprise Shower

Story by Peggy Parish
Pictures by
Barbara Siebel Thomas

based on the original drawings by Fritz Siebel

SCHOLASTIC INC.

New York Toronto London Auckland Sydney
Mexico City New Delhi Hong Kong Buenos Aires

ISBN 0-439-54338-X

Text copyright © 1966 by Margaret Parish.
Text copyright renewed 1994 by the Estate of Margaret Parish.
Illustrations copyright © 1966 by Fritz Siebel.
Illustrations copyright renewed 1994 by the Estate of Fritz Siebel.
Revised illustrations copyright © 1995 by the Estate of Fritz Siebel.
All rights reserved.
Published by Scholastic Inc., 557 Broadway, New York, NY 10012,
by arrangement with HarperCollins Publishers.
SCHOLASTIC and associated logos are trademarks
and/or registered trademarks of Scholastic Inc.

12 11 10 9 8 7 6 5 4 3 2 1   3 4 5 6 7 8/0

Printed in the U.S.A.   23

First Scholastic printing, April 2003

I Can Read Book ® is a trademark of HarperCollins Publishers Inc.

For Stan,
who was born near Alcolu

There was a knock
on the back door.
"Coming, coming,"
called Amelia Bedelia.
She opened the door.

"Oh, it's you, Cousin Alcolu,"

she said. "Do come in."

"Mrs. Rogers asked me

to help out today," said Alcolu.

"Is she having a party or something?"

"Every Tuesday," said Amelia Bedelia,

"some ladies get together.

They just sew and talk.

But today Miss Alma

is in for a real surprise.

Those other ladies

are giving Miss Alma a shower!"

6

"A shower?" said Alcolu.

"A surprise shower!"

said Amelia Bedelia.

"Now why would they do that to her?"

asked Alcolu. "Miss Alma is nice."

"I don't know," said Amelia Bedelia.

"She is about to get married.

They should do something

nice for her.

She can give herself a shower."

"Your folks do have

funny ways," said Alcolu.

9

"Say, are you cooking something?"

"My cupcakes!" said Amelia Bedelia.

She ran to the oven.

"Just right," she said.

"They need to cool a bit.

Then I will ice them."

Mr. Rogers came in.

"Good morning, Amelia Bedelia.

Good morning, Alcolu,"

said Mr. Rogers.

"My, what a nice lot of fish,"

said Amelia Bedelia.

11

"They should taste good," said Mr. Rogers.

"Please scale them and ice them."

"All right," said Amelia Bedelia.

12

"Say, Mr. Rogers, did you ever hear of giving somebody a surprise shower?"

"Oh, yes," said Mr. Rogers.

"It is like a surprise party.

And they shower the person with gifts.

That is why they call it a shower."

Mr. Rogers looked at his watch.

"I have to go to town," he said.

Mr. Rogers left the kitchen.

"By the way, Amelia Bedelia,"

said Alcolu, "Mrs. Rogers told me

to prune the hedge.

Could you show me how?"

"I would be glad to,"

said Amelia Bedelia.

She went to the cupboard.

She took out a box of prunes.

14

Amelia Bedelia and Alcolu

went to the hedge.

"Now," said Amelia Bedelia,

"you take a prune.

Then stick it on like this."

"Is that all there is to it?"

asked Alcolu.

"Prune it well," said Amelia Bedelia.

"Mrs. Rogers likes things done right."

Amelia Bedelia went into the kitchen.

"Oh, I plumb forgot
my cupcakes," she said.

"And I must make that chocolate icing."

Amelia Bedelia put some of this
and a little of that in a big pot.

She stirred and she stirred.

Then she tasted the icing.

"Just right," she said.

Amelia Bedelia began
to ice her cakes.

"The fish!" she said. "Mr. Rogers said

to scale them and ice them."

Amelia Bedelia got the scales.

She piled the fish on them.

"There," she said.

"You just scale yourselves

while I ice the cakes."

18

And Amelia Bedelia iced her cakes.

"Those do look nice," she said.

"And there's enough icing left

to ice the fish too."

Amelia Bedelia picked up

a fish by its tail.

"I hope you have scaled

long enough," she said.

She iced one side of the fish.

Then she iced the other side.

Amelia Bedelia worked

until the last fish was iced.

"That takes care of you," she said.

Amelia Bedelia put the iced fish

and the iced cakes in the cupboard.

Mrs. Rogers came into the kitchen.

"Amelia Bedelia, use this tablecloth

for the table," she said.

"Do run over it first with an iron.

And we need some cut flowers,"

said Mrs. Rogers.

She went out the back door.

Amelia Bedelia unfolded the tablecloth.

She put it on the floor.

Then Amelia Bedelia got the iron.

And she ran all over that tablecloth.

Amelia Bedelia put the tablecloth
on the table.

Alcolu came over to Amelia Bedelia.

"That takes care of that," he said.

"I even had some prunes left.

So I pruned the other bushes too."

"That does look nice," she said.

"Mrs. Rogers will be mighty pleased."

Amelia Bedelia and Alcolu

met Mrs. Rogers at the back door.

Mrs. Rogers came in

with a bunch of flowers.

She put them on the kitchen table.

"Amelia Bedelia," she said,

"use the large silver bowl

for the cut flowers."

"All right," said Amelia Bedelia.

Mrs. Rogers left the kitchen.

She came right back

with a basket of gifts.

"These are for

Miss Alma's shower," she said.

"We will start sewing

as we always do.

Then when all the ladies are here,

we will say, Surprise!

Then comes the shower.

Can you and Alcolu

take care of everything?"

"Oh, yes," said Amelia Bedelia.

"We will see to everything."

"These flowers are so pretty,"

said Amelia Bedelia.

"It's a shame to cut them."

"She said cut flowers," said Alcolu.

"Let me help you."

So Amelia Bedelia and Alcolu

fixed a bowl of cut flowers.

"We do have some

figuring out to do," she said.

"I thought those ladies were

supposed to be giving this shower.

And here *we* are giving it."

"If we had known," said Alcolu,

"we could have fixed up

something fancy."

"It's too late for that now,"

said Amelia Bedelia.

The two of them went outside.

Amelia Bedelia saw the garden hose.

"Think that will do?" asked Alcolu.

"Well, it's not really a shower,"

said Amelia Bedelia.

"But it's the next best thing.

I will give her the gifts

and you can shower her."

"The gifts will get wet," said Alcolu.

"They are shower gifts,"

said Amelia Bedelia.

"What if they do get wet?

We will get wet too."

"Well," said Alcolu.

"We can put on something else."

"What a good idea," said Amelia Bedelia.

"Hide those gifts first," said Alcolu.

Amelia Bedelia hid the basket of gifts

under some bushes.

"It is time to get ready," she said.

A bit later

Amelia Bedelia heard a car stop.

"Here come the ladies,"

she called to Mrs. Rogers.

Mrs. Rogers hurried out to meet them.

Mrs. Ralph came first.

And with her came her four children.

"Look!" they shouted.

"Prunes on the hedge."

The children went racing past.

More and more ladies came.

They began to sew.

But Miss Alma did not come.

"Where is Miss Alma?" everybody asked.

But nobody knew.

Mrs. Rogers looked at the table.

"Footprints!" said Mrs. Rogers.
"Amelia Bedelia, what did
you do to that tablecloth?"
"I ran over it with an iron,"
said Amelia Bedelia. "Should I
have taken my shoes off first?"

39

"Oh, never mind!" said Mrs. Rogers.

"Amelia Bedelia, where are

the cut flowers?" she asked.

"Oh, my," said Amelia Bedelia.

"I forgot them."

Amelia Bedelia ran in

and got the flowers.

Mrs. Rogers looked at the bowl.

"Amelia Bedelia!" she cried.

"What did you do to those flowers?"

"I cut them," said Amelia Bedelia.

"You said to fix a bowl

of cut flowers."

Just then Miss Alma drove up.

"Here she is!" said the ladies.

"Sorry to be late," said Miss Alma.

"But I have a headache."

"I am sorry," said Mrs. Rogers.

"You just sit down."

Mrs. Rogers turned to Amelia Bedelia.

"Are you ready

for the shower?" she asked.

"We will need a minute or two,"

said Amelia Bedelia.

She called Alcolu.

They went around back.

And there stood Amelia Bedelia
and Alcolu in bathing suits.

"All right," called Amelia Bedelia.
"We are ready."

Then all the ladies shouted,

"SURPRISE!"

"SURPRISE!" shouted Amelia Bedelia.

She ran out with the gifts

and dumped them on Miss Alma's lap.

"Here are the gifts," she said.

Alcolu came right behind her

with the hose.

"And here is the shower!" he shouted.

"A shower! A shower!"

screamed Mrs. Ralph's four children.

And they jumped into the shower

with Miss Alma.

48

All the ladies screamed too.

And they jumped out of the shower.

Miss Alma leaped up.

Her gifts flew all over the place.

"How dare you!" she shouted.

Miss Alma was angry.

She was very angry.

"Amelia Bedelia! Alcolu!"

shouted Mrs. Rogers.

"Turn off that water this minute."

Amelia Bedelia and Alcolu

turned off the water.

"Did you see how mad

Miss Alma was?" asked Alcolu.

"I don't think she liked our shower,"

said Amelia Bedelia.

"Maybe some hot tea will help her."

Amelia Bedelia and Alcolu

went into the kitchen.

"I'll take the tea things,"

said Amelia Bedelia.

"You bring the cupcakes.

Here is the tea," said Amelia Bedelia.

"Thank goodness for that,"

said Mrs. Rogers.

"Hmmm, that chocolate looks good," said Mrs. Ralph.

"Help yourself," said Mrs. Rogers.

Mrs. Ralph helped herself

to the biggest piece.

She took her fork.

Mrs. Ralph tried to cut it.

But it would not cut.

And Mrs. Ralph wanted that chocolate.

So she picked it up and bit it.

"Uuggg," she screamed.

"Fish! Raw fish!"

Mrs. Ralph was angry.

She was very angry.

Mr. Rogers came out just then.

He heard what Mrs. Ralph said.

"Fish!" he shouted. "Amelia Bedelia!

What did you do to my fish?"

"Iced them!" said Amelia Bedelia.

Now Mr. Rogers was angry too.

Suddenly Miss Alma started laughing.

Everybody looked at her.

She jumped up and threw her arms

around Amelia Bedelia.

"You are wonderful!"

said Miss Alma.

"My headache is all gone.

That surprise shower

was just what I needed."

Then Mrs. Ralph laughed.

"Amelia Bedelia," she asked,

"did you prune the hedge?"

"Cousin Alcolu did that,"

said Amelia Bedelia.

"Then he is wonderful too,"

said Mrs. Ralph.

"See how happy my children are.

They have never been this good."

And suddenly everybody was laughing.

Mrs. Rogers began

to pour the tea.

Amelia Bedelia served

the chocolate cupcakes.

And the ladies said they were

the best cakes they had ever eaten.

"That was so much fun,"

said all the ladies,

and they laughed some more.

Then they helped pick up

Miss Alma's gifts.

And they were still laughing

when they left.